C000233938

The Firebird

A Play

Neil Duffield

A SAMUEL FRENCH ACTING EDITION

SAMUEL FRENCH

FOUNDED 1830

SAMUELFRENCH-LONDON.CO.UK
SAMUELFRENCH.COM

Copyright © 2004 by Neil Duffield
All Rights Reserved

THE FIREBIRD is fully protected under the copyright laws of the British Commonwealth, including Canada, the United States of America, and all other countries of the Copyright Union. All rights, including professional and amateur stage productions, recitation, lecturing, public reading, motion picture, radio broadcasting, television and the rights of translation into foreign languages are strictly reserved.

ISBN 978-0-573-05136-4

www.samuelfrench-london.co.uk

www.samuelfrench.com

FOR AMATEUR PRODUCTION ENQUIRIES

UNITED KINGDOM AND WORLD
EXCLUDING NORTH AMERICA
plays@SamuelFrench-London.co.uk
020 7255 4302/01

Each title is subject to availability from Samuel French,

depending upon country of performance.

CAUTION: Professional and amateur producers are hereby warned that *THE FIREBIRD* is subject to a licensing fee. Publication of this play does not imply availability for performance. Both amateurs and professionals considering a production are strongly advised to apply to the appropriate agent before starting rehearsals, advertising, or booking a theatre. A licensing fee must be paid whether the title is presented for charity or gain and whether or not admission is charged.

The professional rights in this play are controlled by Samuel French Ltd, 52 Fitzroy Street, London, W1T 5JR.

No one shall make any changes in this title for the purpose of production. No part of this book may be reproduced, stored in a retrieval system, or transmitted in any form, by any means, now known or yet to be invented, including mechanical, electronic, photocopying, recording, videotaping, or otherwise, without the prior written permission of the publisher. No one shall upload this title, or part of this title, to any social media websites.

The right of Neil Duffield to be identified as author of this work has been asserted by him in accordance with Section 77 of the Copyright, Designs and Patents Act 1988

THE FIREBIRD

Commissioned by, and first performed at, The Dukes Theatre, Lancaster on 30th November 2000 with the following cast of characters:

Prince Ivan	Robin Johnson
Tsar Saltan/Wolf/Koschei/Vanka	Patrick Bridgeman
Princess Katya/Baba Yaga	Heather Phoenix
Vasilisa/Pedlar 2	Rachel Colles
The Firebird/Pedlar 1	Deborah Galloway

Directed by Eileen Murphy
Designed by Richard Foxton
Music composed by Rick Juckes
Lighting by Brent Lees
Choreography by Ruth Jones

CHARACTERS

Tsar Saltan
Prince Ivan, his son
Princess Katya, his daughter
Wolf
Koschei the Deathless, a sorcerer
Vasilisa, Princess of Incomparable Beauty, Koschei's
  prisoner
Baba Yaga, a witch
Vanka, Baba Yaga's crow (a puppet)
The Firebird
Pedlar 1, female
Pedlar 2, female
Giant Cloaked Figure

The action of the play takes place in a forest, the Tsar's
palace and garden, Koschei's castle and Baba Yaga's hut

We are in a timeless fantasy land of myth and fairy tale

AUTHOR'S NOTE

There are many different versions of the Firebird story. My own is a combination of several Russian folk tales. The main sources are *The Tale of the Firebird, Tsarevich Ivan and the Grey Wolf; Vasilisa the Beautiful* and *The Frog Princess*. But there are elements of others and sections I've simply invented.

The play uses various kinds of narrative as well as dialogue. It's story-telling children's theatre as opposed to pantomime and relies on situations and characters being played truthfully.

Music may be newly composed for each production. Companies wishing to consider using music from the original Dukes Theatre production, should contact the composer, Rick Juckes at: rick@splashsoundproductions.co.uk. Letters to Mr Juckes will be forwarded to him by Samuel French Ltd; please write to him c/o The Editorial Department.

Neil Duffield

Also by Neil Duffield,
published by Samuel French Ltd

The Secret Garden
adapted from the novel by
Frances Hodgson Burnett

ACT I

A forest

Darkness

The music for Song 1 begins

The Lights come up on the whole cast as a band of cloaked Russian musician pedlars in the forest at night. The actors playing Ivan, Katya and the Tsar wear these characters' costumes under their cloaks. Pedlars 1 and 2 are both female

Pedlar 1 dances. The others play and sing

Song 1

Pedlars (*singing*) La la la
La la la la la la la
La la la la la la la la la
La la la la la la
La la la
La la la la la la la
La la la la la la la la la
La la la la la la

Who will buy
A string of shiny buttons
A silver comb, a looking glass
A rose of ruby
Who will buy
A roll of silken ribbon
A handkerchief of linen
A golden apple for the one you love

Pedlar girl
Dancing in the moonlight
Dancing in the moonlight
Like a bird of fire

Pedlar girl
Weave your magic story
Weave your magic story
Pedlar girl

Who will buy
A scarlet coloured apron
Redder than the horseman of the
Evening sunset
Who will buy
A cloak as black as midnight
Shimmering with starlight
Darker than the horseman of the night

Pedlar girl
Dancing in the moonlight
Dancing in the moonlight
Like a bird of fire
Pedlar girl
Weave your magic story
Weave your magic story
Pedlar girl

Who will buy
A lucky Russian wolf tooth
Wear it round your neck and always
Have good fortune
Who will buy
A polished wooden heart
Shot through with a dart
Keep it as a token of your love

Pedlar girl
Dancing in the moonlight
Dancing in the moonlight
Like a bird of fire
Pedlar girl
Weave your magic story
Weave your magic story
Weave your magic story
Weave your magic story

Pedlar 1 (*speaking*) Imagine a palace. With tall towers and high walls — —

During the following, set elements appear to make the Tsar's palace

Pedlar 2 — and inside that palace a garden.
Pedlar 1 A garden where the trees grow leaves of emerald — —

Set elements appear to create a garden, brought to life by the storytellers

Pedlar 2 — where the bushes blossom with silver and pearl — —
Pedlar 1 — and where the roses bloom with petals of finest ruby.
Pedlar 2 A garden without equal in the length and breadth of Russia.

The Lights change to the setting for the Tsar's garden. Daytime

The actor playing the Tsar removes his pedlar's cloak

Tsar This is the garden of Tsar Saltan, the wealthiest and mightiest ruler in all the thrice nine lands.
Pedlar 2 At the very centre of the garden stands Tsar Saltan's most treasured possession.

An apple tree with golden fruit on it appears

Pedlar 1 An apple tree — bearing fruit of solid gold.
Tsar The most precious possession a Tsar could have.
Pedlar 1 Tsar Saltan guards it with a sharp and jealous eye.
Pedlar 2 Every morning he counts his golden apples to make sure none are missing.
Pedlar 1 And he keeps the garden gate locked and bolted. No-one is allowed to enter — —
Pedlar 2 — except his daughter — —

The actor playing Katya removes her cloak

Katya Princess Katya.
Pedlar 1 — and his son — —

The actor playing Ivan removes his cloak

Ivan Prince Ivan.
Pedlar 2 Every day the Tsar calls them both to him ...
Tsar Ivan! Katya! (*He takes two apples from the tree and hands one each to Ivan and Katya*) I'll give a rose of finest ruby to whoever polishes the brightest apple.

They both go to work

Ivan Every day Ivan polishes as hard as he can.
Katya (*tauntingly*) But he never wins. It's always Katya who gets the rose of finest ruby.

Ivan polishes with increased vigour

Pedlar 2 But as every Pedlar knows, what you need to polish gold — is the tooth of a wolf. (*She takes a wolf's tooth from around her neck and offers it to Ivan*)

Ivan takes the tooth and tries it on the apple; he is encouraged by the result

Katya (*worried*) Katya notices that Ivan's apple is looking shinier than hers. (*She redoubles her efforts*) It's still shinier!

Ivan turns to look at Pedlar 2. Katya takes the opportunity to deftly switch the apples. The Tsar claps his hands to denote the end of polishing. Katya hands her apple to the Tsar

Tsar This is incredible. Look how it shimmers in the light!
Katya Better than Ivan's.

The Tsar examines Ivan's attempt

Ivan I tried. Honestly, Father. I thought I'd done it right this time.
Tsar You never do anything right. You make a mess of everything you touch. The rose of finest ruby goes to Katya.
Pedlar 1 Again.

Ivan gives Pedlar 2 an apologetic look and offers back the tooth

Pedlar 2 (*sympathetically*) Keep it. It may yet bring you luck.

Ivan hangs the tooth round his neck

Katya (*taunting Ivan*) "You never do anything right."

The Tsar becomes agitated

Pedlar 2 But one morning when Tsar Saltan arrives to count his golden apples, he discovers something terrible.

Tsar One of them is missing! One of my golden apples is missing!

Pedlar 1 The next morning the same thing happens again — —

Tsar Another one's gone!

Pedlar 2 — and the morning after that.

Tsar There's a thief in the palace! Someone's stealing all my golden apples!

Pedlar 1 But the garden is locked and bolted.

Pedlar 2 The gate is strong and the walls are high.

Tsar So who could it be?

The Tsar glares suspiciously at the two Pedlars

Pedlars 1 and 2 exit hastily

Katya! Katya!

Katya hurries over to the Tsar

Katya What is it, Father? What's the matter?

Tsar There's a thief in the palace! Someone's stealing my golden apples! You must find out who it is! You must catch them!

Katya Me?

Tsar Tonight. Hide in the bushes and when they show up, jump out and grab them!

Katya What if they don't want to be grabbed? What if they fight back?

Tsar It could be one of the servants — or those pedlars. Don't take your eyes off that tree. Not for a single moment.

Katya Can't Ivan do it?

Ivan Yes, I'll do it, Father! I'll catch the apple thief!

Tsar You couldn't catch a cold. It has to be someone I can trust. Someone who won't let me down. Remember, Katya — you mustn't fall asleep. Not for one moment.

Katya You mean you want me to stay out here? On my own? In the dark?

Tsar All night if you have to.

Katya Can't Ivan even help?

Ivan Please, Father! I won't make a mess of it. Not this time! I promise!

Katya He can do it on his own if he wants!

Ivan Please.

Tsar (*considering*) Very well. He can help. But you do as Katya tells you, do you hear? And if you allow this robber to escape …

Ivan I won't, Father. I won't let you down. Not this time. We'll catch the apple thief, won't we Katya? You can count on us!

The Lights fade. Music plays

   The Tsar exits

Katya and Ivan hide near the tree

The Lights come up on Tsar Saltan's garden. Night-time

The music fades. An owl hoots

Katya and Ivan are both frightened

Katya What was that?
Ivan You don't think it's the apple thief do you?
Katya Have a look.
Ivan Me?
Katya You heard what father said — do as Katya tells you.

Ivan cautiously peers out

Ivan It's too dark. I can't see a thing.
Katya Keep watching.
Ivan What are you going to do?
Katya (*settling down*) I should've been in bed hours ago.
Ivan Father said we mustn't go to sleep. We have to stay awake all night!
Katya There's no point in us both staying awake. (*She rolls over and goes to sleep*)
Ivan Katya — Katya! (*He settles down to wait*) Must stay awake. I mustn't let Father down.

Music plays. A red glow comes up in the sky

   What's that? It's getting lighter — it can't be the dawn. Not yet.

The music and red glow build

   Somebody's coming. Katya! Katya!! (*He tries to wake Katya*)

Katya shrugs Ivan off and goes on sleeping

   Finally, in a blaze of light, the Firebird appears, a fabulous and fantastical creature of brilliant reds and golds. She circles the apple tree in a beautiful whirling dance

Song 2

The Chorus sings, either live or recorded

Chorus (*singing*) Here comes the Firebird
                        Blazing Firebird
                        Blinding Firebird
                        Here comes the Firebird
                        Firebird
                        Setting the heavens aflame
                        Firebird
                        Firebird
Ivan (*singing*)   Tell me who you are
                        With a tail of flame like a shooting star
                        Are you the thief who steals from the Tsar
                        Where is it you come from
                        Firebird

The music underscores the following

Ivan (*speaking*) Katya! Wake up! Katya!
Katya (*grunting*) Leave me alone. Go away.
Ivan The thief! Katya! It's the thief!

We go back into the song

Ivan (*singing*)   Can I catch your flame
                        If I seize your tail will it cause me pain
                        How can I know you're the one to blame
                        Where is it you come from
                        Firebird
Chorus (*singing*) Here comes the Firebird
                        Blazing Firebird
                        Blinding Firebird
                        Here comes the Firebird
                        Firebird
                        Setting the heavens aflame
                        Firebird
                        Firebird

The music underscores the following

The Firebird approaches the apple tree

Ivan (*speaking*) Oh no! What do I do now? Katya! Katya!

The Firebird takes hold of an apple

(*Deciding to act*) Stop! Stop, thief! Stop! (*He rushes towards the Firebird*)

The Firebird takes the apple from the tree and makes to escape

The music swells

There is an exciting chase around the stage. Ivan finally manages to grab the Firebird's tail. The bird continues to flap and flutter during the following with Ivan clinging on for dear life

Firebird Let me go!
Ivan No! I won't! I won't let you go! Katya!
Firebird Let me go, I tell you! Let me go!
Ivan I don't care how much you burn my fingers! Katya!

The Firebird tires and slows down. She realizes there's no escape

You see. I'll hold on to you for ever!
Firebird Please — I beg you. Let me go.
Ivan You're a thief and I'm taking you to my father!
Firebird You don't understand — I have to leave! (*She struggles again*)
Ivan (*clinging on*) Struggle as much as you like, you'll never get away!
Firebird Please. If I stay here I'll die.
Ivan Die?
Firebird I'm the prisoner of Koschei the Deathless. He's a sorcerer. He put a spell on me. If I'm not back by dawn I'll die.
Ivan But I promised Father I'd catch the apple thief.
Firebird Take back your father's golden apple.

The Firebird gives the apple to Ivan

Tell him I'll steal no more. Please. Soon it will be dawn.
Ivan I don't know. (*Pause*) Katya!

Katya sleeps on

The Firebird pulls out one of her feathers

Firebird Give this feather to your father. Tell him the Firebird offers it in return for the golden apples she has already eaten.

Ivan You promise you won't steal any more?
Firebird I shall never again return to his garden.

Ivan cautiously releases the Firebird. She gives him the feather

You've saved my life. I shall take back this feather only to save yours.

Music

The Firebird moves away

The blaze of light recedes

Ivan watches the Firebird go

Song 2 (*reprise*)

The Chorus sings, either live or recorded

Chorus (*singing*) Here comes the Firebird
　　　　　　　　Blazing Firebird
　　　　　　　　Blinding Firebird
　　　　　　　　Here comes the Firebird
　　　　　　　　Firebird
　　　　　　　　Setting the heavens aflame
　　　　　　　　Firebird
　　　　　　　　Firebird

The music ends

Ivan rushes over to Katya

Ivan Katya! Katya! Wake up! Katya!
Katya What is it? What's the matter? What's all the shouting?
Ivan The apple thief! She was here, Katya! The apple thief was here!
Katya What? Where?
Ivan It was a bird! The most beautiful creature you've ever seen. I grabbed
　　her. I burnt my fingers but I clung on. I caught her, Katya. All by myself.
　　I caught the Firebird!
Katya A firebird?
Ivan You should have seen her! She lit up the entire sky!
Katya Where is she? What have you done with her?
Ivan I let her go.
Katya You let her go?

Ivan She would have died. She's the prisoner of a sorcerer — Koschei the
Deathless. He put a spell on her.

Katya You let the apple thief escape?

Ivan She didn't steal anything. Look — here's the apple. And she won't
come back, Katya — she promised. She gave me one of her feathers. She
said I was to give it to Father in exchange for the apples she's eaten.

Katya (*taking the feather*) I'll give the feather to Father.

Ivan Will he be pleased with me, do you think?

Katya Pleased with you? For letting the apple thief escape? I'd start saying
my prayers if I were you.

The Lights fade. Music plays

Ivan exits

The Tsar enters, joins Katya and takes the feather from her

The Lights come up on Tsar Saltan's garden. Daytime

The music fades

The Tsar is examining the feather

Tsar I've never seen anything so fabulous. See how it sparkles! What must
the whole bird be like?

Katya The most beautiful creature on earth. Wings of flame and a tail like
a golden comet.

Tsar Amazing … What's a tree of golden apples compared to a wonder like
that? I must have it, Katya. I want this Firebird here in my garden!

Katya I almost caught it for you. I clung to its tail. It burned my fingers and
scorched my clothes but I didn't let go. I almost had it, a few more moments
— and then …

Tsar Then what?

Katya Then Ivan woke up.

Tsar Ivan? Ivan was sleeping? Through all that commotion Ivan was
sleeping?

Katya I screamed out for him to come and help. I told him to grab the
Firebird's tail to stop it flying away.

Tsar And did he? Did he do as you said?

Katya At first. He grabbed the Firebird by the tail.

Tsar And then?

Katya He let go.

Tsar He let go?

Katya He said it was burning his fingers.

Tsar And the Firebird?

Katya I did my best. I tried to hold on. Then the feather came away in my hand. The Firebird was gone. Soaring into the sky like a meteor.

Tsar (*seething*) That boy. That useless waster of a boy! (*Shouting off*) Ivan! Ivan!

Ivan enters

Ivan (*hopefully*) Here I am, Father. Has Katya told you what I did?

Tsar She told me you let the Firebird escape!

Ivan She won't come back. She won't steal any more golden apples.

Tsar Idiot boy. The Firebird is worth a thousand golden apples. The most precious possession a Tsar could have — and you let it fly off into the night!

Ivan I had to. She would have — —

Tsar You're a failure. I want you out of my sight. I don't want to set eyes on you again.

Ivan Father ...

Tsar I banish you. I banish you from my kingdom. You may return only if you bring back the Firebird you so foolishly lost.

Katya looks triumphant. Ivan glances at Katya and heads out of the palace

There is a lighting change. Music plays

The Tsar and Katya exit

The two Pedlars enter

The set changes back to the forest. One of the trees has a rough sign fastened to it

Ivan leaves his father's kingdom and enters the forest during the following

Pedlar 1 With a sad heart Ivan leaves the palace — —

Pedlar 2 — and the kingdom of his father, Tsar Saltan.

Ivan Will I ever be able to come back home?

Pedlar 1 Where will he go now?

Pedlar 2 What will he do?

Pedlar 1 And what of the Firebird?

Ivan I don't even know where to start looking.

Pedlar 2 The sorcerer.

Pedlar 1 Koschei the Deathless.

Ivan But who is he? Where does he live?

The two Pedlars exit

The Lights come up on the forest

Whether he wanders for a long time or a little, no-one can say. But finally Prince Ivan arrives at the edge of a deep dark forest. (*Reading the sign*) "Go forward and be eaten by wolves. Go back and be a failure." (*He considers his options*) I can't go back — that's for certain — but I don't fancy being eaten by wolves either. (*He struggles with the decision for a moment, then fumbles in his pocket and pulls out a coin. He tosses the coin and glances at the result*) Oh well. At least I won't have to worry about messing things up all the time. (*He sets off in the direction of the forest*)

The Wolf howls, off

Ivan stops dead, pulls out the coin again

Best of three. (*He makes to toss the coin again but stops himself*) No. For once I have to do something right. (*He plucks up his courage and sets off again*)

There is another howl

Ivan stops, wondering whether to turn back. He decides against and continues on his way

The Wolf leaps out from the trees

Wolf Wrrraaah!

Ivan is terrified but somehow manages to stop himself running away. The Wolf tries again

Wrrraaah!!

Ivan still doesn't run away

Can't you read?
Ivan Yes. Very well.
Wolf "Go forward and be eaten by wolves!"
Ivan I know.

Wolf Come this way and be swallowed alive!

Ivan I saw it.

Wolf (*as threateningly as he can*) That means you'll be torn to pieces by a savage bloodthirsty beast!

Ivan (*cringing with fear*) I realize that.

Wolf Then why've you come?

Ivan I tossed a coin.

Wolf Tossed a coin? What's the matter with you? Do you want to be eaten alive?

Ivan No. Not at all.

Wolf I'll give you one last chance to change your mind.

Ivan It's very kind of you, only — —

Wolf Turn back now and, ravenous as I am, I'll let you go.

Ivan Thank you — but I really don't think I can.

Wolf Are you stupid? I'm giving you a second chance. You can change your mind — you can go home!

Ivan I think I'd prefer to be eaten by wolves.

Wolf What?

Ivan I'm enough of a failure as it is.

Wolf Failure's not as bad as you think. Some of the most important people in the world are failures.

Ivan I'm sorry. I've made my decision. (*He prepares to be eaten alive*)

Wolf (*getting desperate*) You could always make a run for it.

Ivan Outrun a wolf?

Wolf I've a bad leg — a very bad leg. Oooohhh! (*He adopts an exaggerated limp*)

Ivan I'd be grateful if you'd get it over as quickly as possible.

Wolf Don't rush me!

Ivan Sorry.

Wolf It's not every day someone wanders into the forest demanding to be eaten alive.

Ivan I thought you were ravenous.

Wolf I am!

Ivan Then what's wrong?

Wolf You're supposed to be terrified!

Ivan I am terrified.

Wolf You're supposed to run through the forest screaming. Then I come howling after you. The scent of blood. The cry of the hunt. All that. (*He howls*)

Ivan Wait a minute. I know what's wrong with you. I can see it now!

Wolf What? What do you mean? What're you talking about?

Ivan You've no teeth! That's why you don't want to eat me, isn't it? You can't! You haven't a tooth in your head!

The Wolf shrinks away in shame

Wolf I suppose you think that's funny, don't you? Think it's hilarious — a wolf with no teeth. Well, go on, enjoy yourself, have a good laugh!

Ivan I don't think it's funny at all.

Wolf A failure — that's what you're thinking, isn't it? A toothless wolf — probably been banished from the pack. Well, as it happens, you're right. That's why I'm out here on my own. So go on, enjoy the joke — have a good laugh!

Ivan To tell you the truth — I might be able to help.

Ivan takes the tooth from around his neck and offers it to the Wolf

Wolf What's that?

Ivan What's it look like?

Wolf It looks like a tooth.

Ivan A wolf's tooth.

The Wolf takes the tooth, examines it and tries it for size

Wolf (*amazed*) It fits — it fits perfectly.

Ivan Keep it. It's yours.

Wolf Mine? You mean it? To keep?

Ivan Not such a failure now, eh?

Wolf I don't know what to say ... I mean I never expected ... Not a tooth, not a real incisor, not an actual fang! How does it look?

Ivan Savage.

Wolf Honest?

Ivan Totally vicious.

Wolf You're kidding. I can't believe it. My own tooth ... I'm a beast again. Lean and mean and fearsome. I could tear you to pieces! I could swallow you whole! (*Quickly*) Oh don't worry — I'm not going to. (*He gives him a hug instead*) I don't know what to say ... Thank you! Thank you! You've transformed my life. You've made me so happy I could dance! In fact I *will* dance!

Music

Song 3

Wolf (*singing*)   Look at me
                      I'm a wolf with a tooth
                      And that's no word of a lie
                      I'm not much use

When I've got no tooth
A wolf with a tooth am I
Owwwwooooo
A wolf with a tooth am I

I can chew I can bite
I can snarl I can fight
I can grind I can gnash I can gnaw
I'm no longer a wolf
With a yawning gulf
The moment I open my jaw
Owwwwoooo
The moment I open my jaw

Wolf ⎫
Ivan ⎭   Look at me
I'm a wolf with a tooth
And that's no word of a lie
I'm not much use
When I've got no tooth
A wolf with a tooth am I
Owwwwoooo
A wolf with a tooth am I

Wolf   I am wild I am rough
I am fierce I am tough
I'm a wolf with an evil eye
No toothless wolf
But a ruthless wolf
A well-fanged wolf am I
Owwwwoooo
A well-fanged wolf am I

Wolf ⎫
Ivan ⎭   Look at me
I'm a wolf with a tooth
And that's no word of a lie
I'm not much use
When I've got no tooth
A wolf with a tooth am I
Owwwwoooo
A wolf with a tooth am I

The music ends

Wolf One good turn deserves another. Tell me what I can do for you —
anything — just say what you want and it's yours!

Ivan It doesn't matter. Honestly.

Wolf I absolutely insist! It's a question of honour — wolf's honour!

Ivan Well actually there is one thing you might be able to — —

Wolf Name it! Doesn't matter what — just name it!

Ivan I'm looking for Koschei the Deathless.

Wolf Koschei?

Ivan I have to rescue the Firebird from him and take her home to my father
… Do you know where he lives?

Wolf How about a parrot? I could get you a fantastic parrot — speaks every
language in the thrice nine lands. Better than a firebird — firebirds are two
a penny!

Ivan You know, don't you? You know where Koschei lives!

Wolf Or a turkey? Think of it — a big fat juicy turkey! Your father'd
welcome you home with open arms!

Ivan Wolf! I have to find him! You promised! Anything I want!

Wolf Even if I told you where he lives, Koschei would never let you take the
Firebird. Forget him — forget the Firebird; you're wasting your time.

Ivan A question of honour, you said — wolf's honour.

The Wolf struggles with the decision

Wolf He lives in a castle. Far away. Beyond the thrice nine lands and the
thrice ten tsardoms.

Ivan Then that's where I must go.

Wolf Koschei's a sorcerer! He's a thousand years old and a thousand times
evil! He'll turn you into a spider and squash you underfoot! Go home!

Ivan Not without the Firebird. (*He moves away*)

Wolf You're not thinking of walking?

Ivan (*stopping*) Is there any other way?

Wolf It's a lifetime's journey!

Ivan Then the sooner I get started the better. (*He moves away again*)

Wolf Wait …

Ivan stops

I'm beginning to think being toothless wasn't so bad after all.

Ivan You mean you'll take me?

The Wolf resigns himself. Ivan is delighted

Wolf Before we go — a word of warning.

Ivan Don't you think you've given me enough already?

Wolf The Firebird is not the only prisoner in Koschei's castle.

Ivan There's someone else?

Wolf Her name is Vasilisa, Princess of Incomparable Beauty.

Ivan (*with immediate interest*) A princess?

Wolf They say the night stars gleam in her eyes, and that her voice sings like the running of a brook. But be warned — you must never look at her.

Ivan A princess of incomparable beauty and I mustn't look?

Wolf Koschei turned her heart to wood. She can love no-one. Not you. Not anyone. Don't look at her. Don't even glance — or you'll be snared by her beauty and trapped forever.

Music, continuing through the following

The Lights cross-fade to a spot

Ivan and the Wolf create a moving image in the spot of Ivan riding on the Wolf's back

The set is changed under the following to the interior of Koschei's castle, with curtained windows, chests of drawers, bottles, potions, books of spells, etc.

Tall mountains, deep lakes, and all the domed cathedrals of Russia flash by; for a wolf travels faster than the wind over the tundra, even with a prince on his back.

Ivan Whether they journey for a long time or a short, no-one can say, but at last Ivan and the Wolf arrive beyond the thrice nine lands and the thrice ten tsardoms — at the castle of Koschei the Deathless.

Ivan and the Wolf exit

The Lights cross-fade to the interior of Koschei's castle

Vasilisa enters and starts searching for something — looking in drawers, behind curtains, etc. After a while she begins to despair

Song 4

Vasilisa (*singing*) I've searched in the corners
I've turned out the drawers
I've looked in the rafters
And under the floors
I've rattled the hinges

And peeped in the locks
I've rolled back the carpet
And looked in the clock
Everywhere
Every way I know how
But oh where oh where oh where
Do I look now
Where do I look now

Does it mean I'm his forever
Does it mean I'm here for good
Does it mean I can't feel love
With a heart that's made of wood

Vasilisa resumes her search

Koschei enters. He is an old wizened sorcerer. He watches Vasilisa for a moment

Vasilisa looks under a cushion

Koschei What are you looking for?

Vasilisa turns round, the cushion in her hand

Trying to find my death, are you? Maybe it's in the lining. Have a look. Go on. Unpick the stitches. Death is a small thing — it could be hidden in the tiniest corner.

Vasilisa puts the cushion down

Perhaps it's in one of the cupboards. Empty the drawers. Search wherever you wish — in a thousand years no-one has found it. Koschei's death is hidden in a place so secret no-one will ever find it.

Vasilisa I will. One day. Then your thousand years will be over.

Koschei And what would become of you, my princess? If I were to die, you would have your wooden heart for ever. Only when you agree to become my bride will I remove the spell and make it beat again.

Vasilisa You think I'd marry a man who keeps me prisoner — who turns my heart to wood so I can feel no joy, no happiness, no love for anyone? I'd sooner have a wooden heart till the day I die ... I hate you!

Koschei Hate as much as you wish. Hate me. Hate the world. Beside hate, love is nothing — something feeble and pathetic. Love is for weaklings. Only the strong know hate. Hate is what binds you and I together.

Vasilisa Nothing on earth could bind me to you.
Koschei Then keep your wooden heart. If you won't love me, then you'll
    love no-one. Look where you will. Open every lid. Empty every jar. You'll
    find my death in none of them.

Koschei exits

Music

Vasilisa I'll never marry you! Never!

Song 4 (*reprise*)

Does it mean I'm his forever
Does it mean I'm here for good
Does it mean I can't feel love
With a heart that's made of wood
(*Her search becomes more frantic*)
I've shaken the cushions
I've looked behind doors
I've lifted the broomstick
And emptied the vase
I've peered up the chimney
And under the stairs
Looked under the table
And felt down the chairs
Everywhere
Every way I know how
But oh where oh where oh where
Do I look now
Where do I look now

Does it mean I'm his forever
Does it mean I'm here for good
Does it mean I can't feel love
With a heart that's made of wood

The music underscores the following

Objects begin to open and shut or move around of their own accord

*Koschei's voice, live or recorded, echoes round the castle like a terrible
nightmare*

Koschei (*voice-over; speaking*) In the drawer, Vasilisa.
                    Behind the clock.
                    Under the broom.
                    On top of the shelf.
                    Under the chair.
                    Look in here, Vasilisa!
                    Behind here, Vasilisa!
                    Under here, Vasilisa!
You'll find my death in none of them ... (*Echoing*) In none of them ... In
none of them .... (*The echoes fade; then his laughter echoes round the
castle*)

The music ends

Vasilisa exits

Ivan and the Wolf appear at the window

Ivan Is this it?
Wolf The castle of Koschei the Deathless.
Ivan I can't see the Firebird.
Wolf Good. Let's get out of here before Koschei comes.
Ivan (*climbing through the window*) She has to be in here somewhere. Aren't
you going to help me look?
Wolf How much do you think one tooth is worth? I'll wait for you here
outside the window.
Ivan What if I get lost? There must be a thousand rooms in this place.
Wolf Take this.
Ivan What?
Wolf It's an invisible thread.
Ivan I can't see anything.
Wolf It wouldn't be invisible if you could see it. (*He offers Ivan the end of
the thread*) Here. Hold the end.

Ivan doubtfully takes the end. The Wolf tugs on it. Ivan instantly jerks forward

Ivan How did you do that?
Wolf Tie it around your waist. If you get lost I'll pull you in.

Ivan ties the invisible thread round his waist and tests it out

And remember, if you meet the Princess of Incomparable — —
Ivan (*interrupting*) I know. Don't look.

Wolf Don't even glance. She can feel no love. Not for you. Not for anyone.
Ivan All right — you told me already.
Wolf And don't forget!

Ivan searches the room while the Wolf feeds out the invisible thread

Vasilisa enters

The Wolf immediately ducks out of sight below the window sill

Vasilisa watches Ivan for a few moments

Vasilisa Are you looking for Koschei's death?
Ivan (*startled*) What?
Vasilisa You won't find it in here. I've searched every corner.

The Wolf appears at the window behind Vasilisa

Ivan You must be Vasilisa — —

The Wolf frantically signals to Ivan to look away

— the Princess of Incomparable … (*The sentence tails off; he stares at Vasilisa*)
Vasilisa Did Koschei bring you here? Has he taken you prisoner too?

The Wolf frantically signals. Ivan waves him away. Vasilisa turns to look. The Wolf ducks out of sight just in time

What is it?
Ivan Nothing. Nothing at all.

The Wolf appears again. Ivan flaps him away a second time

Vasilisa Why do you keep flapping your arm like that?
Ivan My arm? (*He signals even more frantically*)
Vasilisa Your arm. Look at it. It's flapping all over the place.
Ivan Oh that … Flies. It's the flies. (*He swats swarms of imaginary flies*)
Vasilisa I can't see any flies.
Ivan There! Look! There's one! (*He chases the fly madly around the room, swiping in all directions. He falls over and gets up*) Got it! (*He dusts his hands triumphantly*)
Vasilisa What a strange young man.

The Wolf gives a huge tug on the invisible thread. Ivan lurches forward and falls

What's the matter? Are you all right?
Ivan Yes. Yes. Sorry. Very sorry.
Vasilisa You're not drunk are you?

The Wolf gives another tug, and Ivan almost falls again. Vasilisa giggles

Ivan No! You've got to believe me. I'm not drunk. Really I'm n — —

Another tug. Another sharp movement

Stop it, will you!
Vasilisa Stop what?
Ivan Not you. Cut it out!
Vasilisa (*finding it all very amusing*) Who are you? Where've you come from?
Ivan Ivan. I'm Prince Ivan. (*He holds out his hand*)

Vasilisa moves to take Ivan's hand

The Wolf gives another tug and disappears below the window frame, hauling with all his might on the thread. Ivan fights back but is gradually drawn towards the window

Vasilisa is in fits

It's not me! I promise you — this is not me!
Vasilisa Then who is it?
Ivan A wolf! It's the wolf!
Vasilisa You're a wolf?
Ivan Not me! Him! He's the wolf!
Vasilisa Who?
Ivan Pulling the thread!
Vasilisa What thread?
Ivan You can't see it!
Vasilisa You're right, I can't.
Ivan It's invisible! The wolf! In the window!
Vasilisa An invisible wolf!
Ivan No. The thread. In the window. The wolf with the tooth!
Vasilisa (*amused and delighted*) This is unbelievable!
Ivan Stop it, will you! Let me go! (*He is drawn tight up against the window*)

Don't worry. I'll show him. I'll put a stop to this — I'll undo the knot! (*He struggles to untie the thread, finally succeeds and immediately falls flat*)

Vasilisa bursts into giggles

Vasilisa (*helping Ivan up*) Are you all right? Have you hurt yourself?
Ivan (*struggling to re-establish his dignity*) He'll be toothless again once I get my hands on him!
Vasilisa I can't remember the last time I laughed so much.
Ivan I know why he was doing it — he didn't want me to speak to you. He told me not to even look at you. He says you have a wooden heart.

Vasilisa instantly stops laughing and turns away. There is a pause

I didn't believe him. Your heart's not made of wood. I know it isn't.
Vasilisa (*sharply*) Oh you do, do you? And what else do you know about me?!
Ivan That the night stars gleam in your eyes.
Vasilisa What?
Ivan The wolf told me. And that your voice sings like the running of a brook.
Vasilisa (*uncomfortably*) This wolf of yours is a fool. You shouldn't have come here. You should have stayed at home.
Ivan I had to come. I'm looking for the Firebird.
Vasilisa The Firebird?
Ivan I can't go home without her. My father says she's the most precious thing a Tsar could have.
Vasilisa I thought it was Koschei's death you were looking for.
Ivan How can someone's death be hidden?
Vasilisa That's how he's managed to stay alive for a thousand years. No-one can find his death ... But I will ... I have to.
Ivan The wolf was right. You *are* the Princess of Incomparable Beauty.
Vasilisa (*edgily*) You must get away from here — before Koschei finds you. You must leave.
Ivan I can't. Not till I've found the Firebird. (*Cautiously*) And not until you leave with me.
Vasilisa Me?
Ivan I know why you're here. The wolf told me. I can help you escape.
Vasilisa You don't know what you're saying ...
Ivan Once I find the Firebird we'll go together. I can take you with me — on the wolf's back!
Vasilisa You don't understand. It's impossible. I can never come with you. I can never escape from here!
Ivan What do you mean? Why not?

Koschei appears as if by magic

Koschei Because she has a heart of wood. The Princess of Incomparable Beauty feels no love. Not for you. Not for any living being.
Ivan (*backing away*) I don't believe you.
Koschei Tell him, my princess. Tell this young prince what you feel for him.
Vasilisa (*lying*) He means nothing to me.
Koschei You see. Vasilisa feels only hate.
Ivan It's not true. She can feel love. I know she can!
Vasilisa I feel nothing for you! Do you hear? I feel nothing!
Koschei Tell me, Princess, what should I do with this foolish adventurer? Shall I turn him into a toad for your amusement? Or shut him in a barrel and send him to the far side of the moon?
Vasilisa Send him home. The boy bores me.
Koschei But he came to steal you away from me.
Vasilisa No he didn't. He came for the Firebird.
Koschei The Firebird?
Vasilisa He's a foolish prince who thinks he can win his father's love with presents. Send him home.
Koschei So, my young Russian prince, it was the Firebird you came to steal? But I no longer have the Firebird.
Vasilisa What?
Koschei She was stolen by Baba Yaga — the old witch snatched her from the sky. (*An idea occurs to him*) Perhaps this Russian prince could be the one to steal her back.
Vasilisa From Baba Yaga? Look at him — he's a dreamer. Baba Yaga would eat him alive!
Koschei Then nothing would be lost. I wonder: which would you like most, my young prince — the Firebird — or Vasilisa?
Ivan I don't know what you mean.
Koschei Steal the Firebird from Baba Yaga and then you may choose.
Ivan Choose?
Koschei Take the Firebird home to your father — or give her to me.
Ivan Why should I give her to you?
Koschei In return for the Firebird I would remove the spell on Vasilisa. I would give her back her heart.
Vasilisa Don't listen to him! Don't do it!
Koschei She would be free. Free to leave my castle. Free to feel love. The choice is yours, young prince. Vasilisa or the Firebird. But first you have to steal her from Baba Yaga!

Koschei exits, laughing

Vasilisa Don't listen to him! Baba Yaga's a witch! She eats people. Not even Koschei dares tangle with her!

Ivan But she has the Firebird.

Vasilisa Forget the Firebird. Forget both of us. Get away from here! Go home, go anywhere! Never come back!

Ivan I can't leave you. Not here. Not with him!

Vasilisa Don't you see? I can never return what you feel. Koschei's right — I can love no-one!

Ivan You could if he gave you back your heart.

Vasilisa But then you'd lose the Firebird forever — you'd never be able to go home. Don't you see? You can't win. Forget us both. Run away. Run away as far as you can!

Ivan Then I really would be a failure. I'll come back, Vasilisa. I promise you — I'll come back. (*He takes her hand*)

There is a moment of silent communication between them

Ivan climbs out through the window and exits

Vasilisa watches Ivan go

Vasilisa Take care, my funny little prince. Take care.

Music

As she watches Ivan disappear into the night, a tiny green bud bursts from Vasilisa's wooden heart. What will become of her prince? Will he steal back the Firebird. And if so, who will he choose? Her — or his father? But worst of all …

Baba Yaga enters; a spotlight comes up on her

Baba Yaga What if he should fall into the clutches of Baba Yaga? (*She laughs*)

Black-out

ACT II

The forest and the exterior of Baba Yaga's hut on chicken legs

Darkness

Music plays

A spotlight comes up on Ivan and the Wolf in a moving image of Ivan riding on the Wolf's back

During the course of the following journey we see three galloping horsemen (puppets) in the sky above them — representing day, evening and night

Wolf Over white-topped mountains, over blue lakes and green forests fly Ivan and the Wolf.
Ivan Past the golden horseman of day — —
Wolf — past the blood-red horseman of evening — —
Ivan — until finally the dark horseman of night gallops by, wrapping the earth in his cloak of black and studded diamonds.
Wolf At the heart of the darkest forest in all of Russia stands a hut on giant chicken legs. Ivan and the Wolf have arrived at the home of Baba Yaga.

The Lights come up slowly on the forest and the hut at night

Ivan This must be the most terrible place on earth. No wonder Koschei didn't dare come himself.
Wolf Not even a wolf at full moon would venture into this part of the forest. Baba Yaga may have bad eyes but her nose is as sharp as a bloodhound's.
Ivan Do you think she's in there?
Wolf Who knows? You're never sure where Baba Yaga is.
Ivan Then maybe the hut is empty.
Wolf She has a guard — an old black-hearted raven called Vanka. If he sees you he'll set up such a screeching and a squawking that Baba Yaga will be back in seconds.
Ivan So what are we going to do?
Wolf Forget the whole thing and get out of here.

Ivan I'll go alone. If the Firebird's in there I should have no trouble finding
her. (*He heads towards the hut*)

Wolf Before you go — a word of warning.

Ivan Not another?

Wolf The Firebird will be fastened by a golden cord. Bring the Firebird but
leave behind the golden cord.

Ivan Why can't I take the cord?

Wolf Don't even try. Untie the Firebird and leave the cord behind. Whatever
you do, don't try to take it!

Ivan All right — I get the message.

Wolf And this time, don't forget!

The Wolf exits

Music

*During the following the exterior of Baba Yaga's hut opens up to reveal the
interior. The hut contains Baba Yaga, asleep and snoring, Vanka, a large
puppet crow, sleeping, and the Firebird, awake, tied by a golden cord to
Vanka's leg. Among the objects in the room is a broom*

Ivan   Witch's hut
                        On chicken legs
                        Stop your dancing
                        Stop your prancing
                        Witch's hut
                        On chicken legs
                        Come up close
                        Come up close
                        And open wide
                        Witch's hut
                        On chicken legs
                        Let us see
                        What lies inside

The music continues, underscoring the following

Ivan pushes the door open. It squeaks. He cautiously enters the hut

Baba Yaga and Vanka both grunt and stir. The Firebird sees Ivan

Sshhh. (*He makes his way on tiptoe across the room*)

There is plenty of suspense, underscored by the music

(*Finally reaching the Firebird; whispering*) Now to unfasten the cord. (*He starts to untie it, then stops. Whispering*) Wait a minute. If I undo this there'll be nothing to stop you flying away. Wolf's warnings make no sense … I'll take it.

Firebird (*too late*) No!

Ivan pulls on the cord only to discover that the other end is tied to Vanka's leg. Vanka starts to flap wildly, screeching and squawking at the top of his voice. There are a few seconds of chaos and cacophony

Vanka Kwaaa! Kwaaa! Kwaa! Kwaaa! Kwaaa! Kwaa!

Baba Yaga wakes up and sniffs the air

Baba Yaga   Who is it? Who's there?
                       Not a raven.
                       Not a witch.
                       I smell the blood of a Tsarevitch!
                       (*She locks the door*)
                       No room to run.
                       No place to hide.
                       The door is locked.
                       The Russian prince is trapped inside.
                       (*She sets off in pursuit of Ivan*)
                       My eyes are bad
                       But my nose is good
                       I smell the scent
                       Of a prince's blood!
                       (*She makes a grab at him*)

Ivan evades Baba Yaga and there is a short chase around the hut, Baba Yaga sniffing and grabbing, Vanka squawking and pecking. Finally Baba Yaga grabs Ivan

                       Got you!
                       Now there's no escape
                       The time has come
                       To meet your fate!
                       (*She fingers his arm*)
                       A tender arm
                       Young and fresh.
                       Soon I'll dine
                       On Russian flesh.

Baba Yaga ties Ivan up during the following

> Tie the knot
> And tie it tight
> Keep you till
> Tomorrow night
> Light the fire
> And burn it hot
> Then roast you
> In my cooking pot!
> (*She laughs*)

Music. During the following song, Vanka dances along and keeps trying to join in, much to Baba Yaga's annoyance

Song 5

Baba Yaga (*singing*) You'll wish you'd never heard of the Firebird
> You'll rue the day you came this way
> There's no way out
> There's no escape
> Right here for good you'll stay

Vanka Kwaaa kwaa!

Baba Yaga aims a swipe at Vanka with her broom

Baba Yaga (*speaking*) I'll do the singing, thank you!
> (*Singing*) This time tomorrow night the stove I'll light
> Stoke it well, get the fire hot
> Some olive oil
> Bring to the boil
> Then you go in my pot

Vanka Kwaaa kwaa!

Baba Yaga (*aiming another angry swipe at Vanka; speaking*) Didn't you hear! I'm the one who does the singing!
> (*Singing*) I eat slugs and snails and rats
> I eat lizards I eat bats
> I'm a most discriminating gastronome
> But what I like the most
> Is a slice of princely roast
> And the taste of lovely juicy Russian bones

Vanka opens his mouth. Baba Yaga threatens him with the broom

(*Speaking*) Don't even think about it!
    (*Singing*) There's no taste known like a Russian bone
          Cooked just right to whet the appetite
          I can hardly wait
          To have you on my plate
          Then I take my first bite

Vanka (*enthusiasm getting the better of him*) Kwaaa kwaaa kwaaa!

Baba Yaga loses her temper and thrashes Vanka with the broom during the following

Baba Yaga (*speaking*) How many times do I have to say it! No singing! No singing! No singing!!

The music underscores as the beating continues

The hut closes up again

The Lights cross-fade to a spot on the Wolf

Wolf Outside in the forest the Wolf hears the clamour and the clatter and the shouting and the squawking and realizes what has happened. Why does he never listen? Oh, fool that I am! Oh, stupid, grey toothless fool that I am! Why did I bring him here? Why did I let him go?

The music speeds up

The Wolf forms a moving image in the spot. This time the speech and journey are much more hurried. The puppets of the three horsemen speed across the sky

During the following, a shuttered window is placed on stage

Vasilisa enters and stands behind the window

          Back over white-topped mountains.
          Back over blue lakes and green forests.
          Past the golden horseman of day.
          Past the blood-red horseman of evening.
          Past the dark horseman of night wrapping the earth in his
             cloak of black and studded diamonds.
          Beyond the thrice nine lands and the thrice ten tsardoms.
          All the way back to the castle of Koschei the Deathless ...

The music ends

The Wolf arrives outside the shuttered window, gasping for breath. He knocks on the shutters

The shutters open and we see Vasilisa beyond them

Vasilisa Wolf! Are you alone? Where's Ivan?
Wolf Terrible news. The worst — the absolute worst!
Vasilisa What is it? What's happened to him?
Wolf Take the Firebird, I said, but leave behind the golden cord!
Vasilisa What golden cord? What are you talking about?
Wolf Does he take any notice? Does he ever take one single scrap of notice?
Vasilisa Wolf! Just tell me! What's happened!?
Wolf It's this tooth. I should never have accepted it. It's my own fault! Oh misery, misery!
Vasilisa Is he dead?
Wolf Worse. Much worse!
Vasilisa Worse?!
Wolf Doomed! Beyond hope! She probably has the stove already lit!
Vasilisa Then he might still be alive?
Wolf The thought of Baba Yaga picking over his bones! Oh misery misery misery!
Vasilisa Quick! There's no time to lose!
Wolf What?
Vasilisa We have to go!
Wolf Go where?
Vasilisa To rescue Ivan!
Wolf You mean — back there ... Back to — —
Vasilisa I'll ride on your back. Come on. Hurry!

Music

The Lights cross-fade to a spot

Vasilisa and the Wolf create a moving image in the spot of Vasilisa riding on the Wolf's back

The travelling sequence now takes place at top speed; the puppets zip past in confusion and disorder

Wolf   White-topped mountains. Blue lakes. Green forests.
                           Golden horseman of the day

	Blood-red horseman of ...
	Dark shadowed horseman wrapping ...
	Thrice nine ... thrice ten ...
	All the way back to the darkest forest in — —
Vasilisa	— the home of Baba Yaga.

Vasilisa climbs off the Wolf's back. The Wolf collapses with exhaustion

The music ends

Thank you, grey brother. You've done me a great service.
Wolf It's what I've done to myself that bothers me.
Vasilisa Now for Baba Yaga.
Wolf Can't we think about this? Baba Yaga's an ogress: she eats people —
and wolves!
Vasilisa I'll disguise myself as a pedlar.
Wolf She eats them too!
Vasilisa I'll go alone.
Wolf You mean you don't want me to ...
Vasilisa Hide. Here in the trees.
Wolf Oh thank you! Thank you, thank you, thank you!!

The Wolf dashes off to hide

Music

*Baba Yaga's hut opens up during the following. Ivan is in the hut, still tied
up, and Baba Yaga is preparing her cooking pots*

Vasilisa	Witch's hut
	On chicken legs
	Come up close
	And open wide
	Let us see
	What lies inside

The music ends

Vasilisa exits

The Lights come up on the hut

Baba Yaga sings as she prepares her pots

Song 6 (*reprise of Song 5*)

Baba Yaga (*singing*) I eat slugs and snails and rats
                       I eat lizards I eat bats
                       I'm a most discriminating gastronome
                       But what I like the most
                       Is a — —

Vasilisa enters with a basket and knocks on the hut door

Baba Yaga stops and sniffs the air

         (*Speaking*) My eyes are bad
                       But my nose is good
                       I smell the scent
                       Of more Russian blood.

Baba Yaya opens the door and Vasilisa enters the hut

Vasilisa Shiny buttons, Grandmother? A silver comb for your hair?
Baba Yaga Who are you?
Vasilisa Just a pedlar girl, Grandmother. A roll of ribbon? A linen handkerchief? How about a ruby rose to bring you fortune?
Baba Yaga (*grabbing Vasilisa's arm and feeling it*) Skin and bone. Not an ounce of good meat ... What sort of pedlar are you?
Vasilisa A hard-working one, Grandmother. I can mend, I can sew, I can polish ... If you don't mind my saying, your hut could do with a good dusting.
Baba Yaga Insolent saucepot — there's no dust in my hut!
Vasilisa Then I'll polish your boots. Or darn your stockings.
Baba Yaga Can you cook?
Vasilisa Have you heard of a pedlar girl who couldn't?
Baba Yaga Can you cook a Russian prince?
Vasilisa Roasted or casseroled? If you like I could add a sprinkle of rosemary to bring out the flavour and serve him up in a creamy white wine sauce.
Baba Yaga (*her mouth beginning to water*) With carrots and turnips?
Vasilisa Delicately braised in rich goats' cheese and garnished with fresh parsley and baked apple.
Baba Yaga Perhaps I could use a little help.
Vasilisa You needn't lift a finger, Grandmother. I shall cook him and serve him up to you in style ... But first you need a new headscarf.

Baba Yaga Headscarf?

Vasilisa I don't wish to offend, Grandmother. But the one you're wearing doesn't do you justice.

Baba Yaga It doesn't?

Vasilisa A style-conscious woman should be seen in a scarf that complements her beauty. If you were to ask my opinion, I would suggest gold.

Baba Yaga Gold?

Vasilisa As dazzling as the noonday sun. I could make it for you in no time.

Baba Yaga Perhaps this one *is* looking a little worn.

Vasilisa Rest your bones, good Grandmother. When you awake your golden headscarf will be waiting.

Baba Yaga starts dropping off almost instantly

Baba Yaga If you're thinking you can run away …

Vasilisa Sleep, Grandmother. Relax and sleep.

Baba Yaga Guard her well, Vanka. (*She falls asleep and snores*)

Ivan Vasilisa.

Vasilisa Ivan.

Ivan Why did you come here? She'll eat us both now!

Vasilisa Not if I can help it.

Ivan What happens when she wakes up and finds there's no golden headscarf?

Vasilisa But she will find a golden headscarf.

Ivan How are you going to do that?

Vasilisa We have a friend to help us.

Music

The Golden Horseman of Day (puppet) appears in the sky above them

Song 7

> (*Singing*) Golden horseman
> Horseman of the day
> Golden horseman
> Galloping on high
> Golden horseman
> Throw down from the sky
> Your cloth of gold

A gold cloth flutters down from the sky. Vasilisa catches it

The music ends

Vanka instantly raises the alarm

Vanka Kwaaa! Kwaaaa! Kwaaaaa! Kwaaaaaaa!

Baba Yaga jumps up and rushes round the room

Baba Yaga Where is she? Where's she gone? Wait till I get my hands on the skinny little hussy! I'll boil her bones!
Vasilisa Calm yourself, Grandmother, calm yourself. I'm here. I've been here all the time.
Baba Yaga Then why did Vanka wake me up? Why did he sound the alarm?
Vasilisa He was singing, that's all. Only singing.
Vanka (*trying to protest his innocence*) Kwaaa! Kwaaa!
Baba Yaga Singing, was he? I'll give him singing! (*She picks up the broom and gives Vanka a hefty swipe*)
Vanka (*pained*) Kwaaaa!
Baba Yaga How many times have I told you? I do the singing around here! (*To Vasilisa*) Where's my headscarf? You promised me a golden headscarf!
Vasilisa And I keep my promises, Grandmother. (*She shows the scarf to Baba Yaga*)

Baba Yaga examines the scarf with her short-sighted eyes

Baba Yaga It is gold.

Vasilisa puts the scarf on to Baba Yaga

Vasilisa There. Now you look like an empress.
Baba Yaga An empress? (*She admires herself*) I like it. I like it a lot. I'll dine like an empress too. Cook me that Russian prince!
Vasilisa Gladly, Grandmother. But first you need a new apron.
Baba Yaga New apron? Why should I need a new apron?
Vasilisa Would an empress dine in an apron full of patches? A woman of fashion should be seen in an elegant apron. A scarlet apron.
Baba Yaga Scarlet?
Vasilisa As red as blood. I could make it for you in no time.
Baba Yaga Perhaps this one is looking a little worn.
Vasilisa Rest your bones, good Grandmother. When you awake your blood-red apron will be waiting.
Baba Yaga Guard her well, Vanka. And this time, no singing! (*She falls asleep and snores*)

Ivan What now? Where are we going to find a blood-red apron?
Vasilisa We have more friends than you know.

Music

Song 7 (2)

The Blood-red Horseman of Evening (puppet) appears in the sky above them

> (*Singing*) Blood-red horseman
>   Horseman of the dusk
>   Blood-red horseman
>   Galloping on high
>   Blood-red horseman
>   Throw down from the sky
>   Your cloth of red

A red cloth flutters down from the sky. Vasilisa catches it

The music ends

Once again Vanka immediately sounds the alarm

Vanka Kwaaa! Kwaaaa! Kwaaaaa! Kwaaaaaa!

Baba Yaga jumps up

Baba Yaga Where is she? Where's she gone? Wait till I get my hands on the little stick insect! I'll boil her bones!
Vasilisa Calm yourself, Grandmother, calm yourself. I'm here. I've been here all the time.
Baba Yaga Then why did Vanka sound the alarm? Why did he wake me up?
Vasilisa He was singing, that's all. Only singing.
Baba Yaga Singing? Again!
Vanka (*desperately protesting his innocence*) Kwaaaaaa! Kwaaaaaa! Kwaaaaaaa!

Baba Yaga picks up the broom

Baba Yaga Didn't I tell you?! No more singing! (*She thrashes Vanka mercilessly*) No — more — singing!
Vanka (*in pain and anguish*) Kwaaaa.
Baba Yaga Where's my apron? You promised me a scarlet apron!

Vasilisa And I keep my promises, Grandmother.

Vasilisa helps Baba Yaga to put on the new apron

> As red as blood.

Baba Yaga It makes me hungry just to look at it. Time to cook that Russian prince!

Vasilisa Almost, Grandmother. First you need a new cloak.

Baba Yaga Cloak?

Vasilisa A cloak of black and studded diamonds. As dark and deep as the night itself — the cloak of an enchantress.

Baba Yaga An enchantress?

Vasilisa I could make it for you in no time.

Baba Yaga Perhaps this one *is* looking a little worn.

Vasilisa Rest your bones, good Grandmother. When you awake your cloak of black and studded diamonds will be waiting.

Baba Yaga Guard her well, Vanka — and if you should dare to sing so much as one single note, I'll thrash you till you've not a feather left! (*She falls asleep and snores*)

Ivan Not another friend?

Vasilisa Of course.

Music

The Dark Horseman of Night (puppet) appears above them in the sky

Song 7 (3)

Vasilisa (*singing*) Diamond horseman
> Horseman of the night
> Diamond horseman
> Galloping on high
> Diamond horseman
> Throw down from the sky
> Your cloth of night

A black, star-studded cloth flutters down from the sky

Vanka hops up and down in silent frustration

Vanka (*stifled*) Kwaa.

Vasilisa (*jabbing a finger at him*) Remember! Not one single note!

Vanka remains silent — with difficulty

Vasilisa drapes the black cloak over the sleeping Baba Yaga

Vasilisa I keep my promises, good Grandmother. As dark and deep as the night itself.

Vasilisa carefully steals the key to the door and unties Ivan

Vanka jumps and hops in utter frustration

    (*Warning Vanka*) You won't have a feather left.

Vasilisa frees Ivan. They give each other a silent hug. They tiptoe to the door. Vasilisa unlocks it and they make to exit

Ivan (*remembering*) Wait — the Firebird. (*Completely forgetting himself, he pulls at the golden cord*)
Firebird (*too late*) No!
Vanka (*jerked by the cord*) Kwaaa! Kwaaa! Kwaa! Kwaaa! Kwaaa! Kwaa!

Ivan quickly frees the Firebird

Baba Yaga wakes and starts to thrash around under the cloak of black and studded diamonds

Vasilisa Run!

Ivan, Vasilisa and the Firebird make a dash for it. Baba Yaga sets off after them. There is a wild chase

During the chase, the hut setting is removed

Finally Ivan, Vasilisa and the Firebird manage to escape from Baba Yaga

    Baba Yaga exits

The Lights come up on the forest

Ivan That was close.
Vasilisa She won't be fooled for long. You must leave — straight away.
Ivan Leave? What're you talking about?
Vasilisa Take the Firebird. Go home. Quickly!
Ivan Not without you. I'm not leaving without you.
Vasilisa There's no time to argue. Hurry!
Ivan Come with me. Back to my father's kingdom. We'll go together.
Vasilisa It's no use. I told you before — I can't feel what you feel!

Ivan You can! I know you can!

Vasilisa Don't you see? I have a heart of wood. I can't love you. I can never love you!

Koschei appears by magic

Koschei …

Koschei Congratulations, young prince. I see you have stolen back the Firebird. So now you must choose what to do with her. Take her home to your father — or give her to me.

Vasilisa Take her to your father! You have to!

There is a pause. Ivan wrestles with the decision

Koschei Which is more important? The respect of your father? Or the heart of a princess you hardly know?

Vasilisa Take her to your father! It's why you came here!

Ivan What will happen to you then?

Vasilisa It doesn't matter! Take the Firebird! You can never go home without her!

Ivan (*turning to the Firebird*) Tell me, what should I do with you? I don't know what's right. Which should I choose?

Firebird Only you can answer that, Prince Ivan.

Ivan struggles for a few moments more, then makes up his mind

Ivan I choose Vasilisa! (*He hands over the Firebird's golden cord to Koschei*) The Firebird is yours. Now do as you promised … Give Vasilisa her heart.

Koschei starts to chuckle

What's the matter? Why are you laughing?

Koschei Foolish prince. Foolish love-sick prince!

Ivan I've given you the Firebird — I've made my choice!

Koschei And you will regret it for ever. The Princess of Incomparable Beauty will never love you.

Ivan You said you'd give her back her heart! You promised!

Koschei Promises are for fools. Take your princess. Enjoy your misery together. Her heart will remain wooden for ever. As will yours!

Music plays suddenly. Koschei points a finger at Ivan's heart. Ivan reels backwards in pain

Ivan What are you doing?

A special lighting effect comes up

Koschei   Spell of evil
                     Keen and sharp
                     Give this prince
                     A wooden heart!

The music builds

Vasilisa No! Koschei! Please! I'll be your bride! I'll do whatever you want!
Koschei   Take this heart
                     Of prince's blood
                     And turn it into
                     One of wood!
Vasilisa No! Koschei! Not Ivan! No! No! (*She bursts into tears*)

Koschei immediately steps back in horror

The music hangs in the air

Koschei Stop! Stop it I tell you. Stop that crying!

The music starts to build again but with a completely different feel

(*Pointing in terror at Vasilisa's cheek*) There. On your cheek — a tear! You have a wooden heart — it isn't possible!

The music continues to build and the Lights change

A giant cloaked figure of Death appears and draws Koschei in towards it. At the same time Koschei shrivels and shrinks with age

Death. Not death! It can't be! I'm Koschei! I'm destined to live for ever! I'm Koschei!

Koschei finally disappears into the cloaked figure of Death

  Death exits with Koschei

The music softens and the Lights return to normal

Ivan So that's where his death was hidden — in one of your tears.

We hear a soft heartbeat within the music

Vasilisa Ivan … My heart — I think it's beating …

The beat in the music grows

It is … I can feel it! Ivan, it's beating! My heart is beating!

The music builds. They embrace. There is a moment of joy and celebration

A wooden heart appears above the set and glows with life

The music ends

Ivan Now will you come with me?
Vasilisa Yes. Yes, I will — and we'll take the Firebird with us!
Ivan No — not the Firebird.
Vasilisa What do you mean?

Ivan unties the golden cord and releases the Firebird

Ivan Fly where you will, my beautiful bird. You're free.
Firebird Once before you set me free.
Ivan And I was right. You belong to no-one. Not to Koschei. Not to Baba
    Yaga. And not to my father.
Firebird May I fly wherever I choose?
Ivan Anywhere — in all the thrice nine lands and the thrice ten tsardoms.

*Music plays. The Firebird flutters around for a few moments trying out her
freedom, then returns to Ivan*

Firebird Then I shall fly with you. To the garden of Tsar Saltan.
Ivan I've no right to ask that of you.
Firebird It's what I choose.
Vasilisa Then we'll go together! All three of us!

They set off

Ivan Wait a minute. How are we going to get there?

  The Wolf enters

Wolf Owwwwoooo!

They all laugh

Music plays; the Lights cross-fade to a spotlight. The actors create a moving image of Ivan and Vasilisa on the Wolf's back with the Firebird flying alongside

During the following the set changes to Tsar Saltan's palace and garden

Tall mountains, deep lakes, and all the domed cathedrals of Russia flash by; for a wolf travels faster than the wind over the tundra — even with a prince and a princess on his back!
Ivan Whether they journey for a long time or a short, no-one can say …
Firebird But at last, far in the distance, they see a palace. With tall towers and high walls.

They break the image and each bids goodbye to the Wolf

The Wolf exits

Ivan   Inside that palace is a garden.
                           A garden where the trees grow leaves of emerald.
                           Where the bushes blossom with silver and pearl.
                           And where the roses bloom with petals of finest ruby.
                           A garden without equal in the length and breadth of
                               Russia.

Ivan, Vasilisa and the Firebird exit

Katya enters the garden wearing gloves

The Lights come up on the Tsar's garden. The music ends

Katya produces a tin of polish and a cloth. She takes a golden apple from the tree and reads from the lid of the tin

Katya (*reading*) "Apply polish to surface of apple. Avoid contact with skin."
(*With extreme caution she smears some polish on the cloth and applies it to the apple. She polishes the apple. Reading*) "Replace apple on tree." (*She replaces it. Reading*) "Repeat with rest of apples." (*She takes down another apple and sets to work polishing it*)

The Tsar enters. He's gloomy and lost in thought and hardly notices Katya

Katya Father.

The Tsar doesn't respond

You'll never guess what I'm doing …

Tsar You're polishing the apples. You're always polishing the apples.

Katya But this time it's different. This is special polish. Very special polish. (*She hands the tin to the Tsar*)

Tsar (*reading from the lid*) Poison?

Katya In case of apple thieves. Any thief who touches this apple with his bare hands will be dead in seconds.

Tsar Are you sure that's wise?

Katya We'll never have to worry about them being stolen again. I'm doing them all.

Tsar I used to think my golden apples were the most precious possession a Tsar could have.

Katya They are. And this will make sure no-one takes any.

Tsar (*picking up the Firebird's feather*) Then I thought the Firebird was even more precious.

Katya You have to stop thinking about the Firebird. It's gone. It's gone for ever.

Tsar I was wrong, Katya. Golden apples are not the most precious thing a Tsar could have. Nor is the Firebird.

Katya What do you mean?

Tsar Nothing on earth is worth the loss of a son.

Katya Ivan?

Tsar I said terrible things to him. I was wrong. I should never have sent him away.

Katya But he was a failure. He let you down.

Tsar I let him down. And now he's gone for good.

The Tsar exits

Katya vents her frustration

Ivan (*off*) Father? … Father!
Katya Ivan?

Ivan enters with Vasilisa and the Firebird

Ivan (*pleased to see her*) Katya … I'm back … I've come home. Vasilisa, this is my sister, Katya.

Katya (*ignoring Vasilisa*) The Firebird? You caught the Firebird?

Ivan She came of her own free will ... Where's Father?

Katya Busy. He's very busy ...

Ivan But he'll want to see the Firebird, I know he will. Father!

Katya Wait! You can't see him. He left strict instructions.

Ivan Is he still angry with me?

Katya More than ever. He said he never wants to see you again.

Ivan But he'll forgive me when he sees the Firebird.

Katya (*stalling*) Look. Let me talk to him first — he'll listen to me. I'll try and persuade him to see you.

Ivan Would you?

Katya (*moving to take the Firebird*) I'll take the Firebird.

Vasilisa stops Katya

Vasilisa You should show the Firebird to your father yourself, Ivan.

Ivan You don't know what he's like. Katya's right — it's best she talks to him.

Katya tries again to take the Firebird. Again Vasilisa stops her

Vasilisa Ivan. You must talk to your father yourself.

Katya You're not going to listen to a pedlar, are you?

Ivan hesitates

Ivan I don't know. Maybe Vasilisa's right.

Katya She's trying to trick you. She wants the Firebird for herself!

Ivan No. No, she's right. I have to face up to Father myself.

Katya (*furiously*) Very well. In that case I'll go and get him ... Perhaps your pedlar girl could finish polishing this apple for me. (*She hands Vasilisa the apple*)

Music underscores the following

Vasilisa It feels strange ... My hands ... What is it? What's happening?

Ivan What's the matter? Vasilisa! What's wrong?

Vasilisa The apple. There's something on it. Something's happening. I feel ...

Ivan snatches the apple from Vasilisa

Ivan What is it? Katya! What's wrong with her?!

Katya It serves her right! It serves you both right!

Ivan Vasilisa! Vasilisa!

Vasilisa dies

What have you done to her? Katya, what have you done?
Katya So touching. The prince and his pedlar.
Ivan Katya ... (*He dies*)
Katya Sleep, little brother. Sleep for ever.

The music ends

Tsar Saltan enters

Tsar Katya? I thought I heard voi — — (*He stops in horror*) Ivan? Ivan!
What's wrong? What's the matter with him?
Katya He's dead ... They're both dead.
Tsar Dead?
Katya They touched one of the poisoned apples. They were trying to steal
it for the Firebird.
Tsar (*seeing the Firebird for the first time*) The Firebird?
Katya They stole that too. They were keeping it for themselves!
Tsar (*to the Firebird*) You? My son died because of you?
Katya It was them all along — Ivan and the Pedlar — they were trying to
steal everything from you!
Tsar (*to the Firebird*) Is this true?
Katya I saw them. I came in and saw them!
Firebird If you want to know the truth, Tsar Saltan — ask the children.
Katya Don't listen to her! It was them I tell you! They were stealing your
golden apples!
Tsar (*to the audience*) Is this true? Were they stealing the golden apples?

The audience is encouraged to respond

Then what happened?

The audience is encouraged to respond

Katya? Katya gave them the poisoned apple?
Katya They're lying! Don't listen to them! They're all liars!
Tsar You? It was you? He was your brother ... You poisoned your own
brother! (*He collapses in grief*) Ivan ... Ivan!
Firebird Tsar Saltan. When I first came to your garden Ivan saved my life.
In return I gave him a feather.

Tsar I still have it. It's here.

Firebird I promised that if ever I took back that feather it would be to save
Ivan's life.

Tsar It's too late. He's dead. They're both dead!

Firebird Give me the feather.

The Tsar gives the feather to the Firebird. She replaces it in her tail

With this feather I shall fly to the ends of the earth — to the fountain of life.

Music plays and the Lights change

*The Firebird takes flight. She flies on her journey to the ends of the earth in
a beautiful combination of music and dance*

*The Firebird reaches her destination. A spectacular fountain of colour and
light cascades over her*

The Firebird makes her return journey, the music and dance continuing

The Lights return to normal

*The Firebird returns to the Tsar's garden and pours a drop of water each
over the eyes of Ivan and Vasilisa*

Firebird Water of life. Touch these eyes and let them see the world anew.

The music swells. Ivan and Vasilisa slowly come back to life

Ivan Father?

*There is a moment of uncertainty. Tsar Saltan stares in amazement, unable
to speak*

I came back …I wanted you to see the Firebird.

Tsar Ivan …

Ivan I wanted to show you I'm not a failure.

Tsar What have I done? All these years. Oh my son, what have I done?

Ivan You're not angry with me?

Tsar Angry? I'm the happiest Tsar in the world!

The Tsar takes Ivan in his arms

I thought the most precious possession a Tsar could have must be made of gold — or feathers of flame. Now I know. A Tsar who loses his son is the poorest man on earth. (*To Katya*) But as for you! You lied. You cheated. You even tried to kill. You're a selfish and wicked girl and I never want to set eyes on you again. I banish you! I banish you from my kingdom!

Katya turns to go

Ivan Father ...

Tsar She's done terrible things! She has to be punished!

Vasilisa Tsar Saltan, rather than banish your daughter, why not let her learn a different life.

Tsar What kind of life?

Vasilisa produces a pedlar's cloak from a hiding place on the set

Vasilisa The life of a pedlar.

Katya A pedlar!

Tsar Now there's an idea.

Katya Father! I can't be a pedlar! Pedlars are poor! They go knocking on doors — selling buttons — in the snow ... I'm a princess! I'm Princess Katya!

The Tsar wraps the pedlar's cloak around Katya

Tsar Now you're just Katya — Katya the Pedlar!

The others all enjoy Katya's discomfort

Ivan (*after a moment*) You know, I think I wouldn't mind being a pedlar.

Tsar You?

Ivan finds a pedlar's cloak in the same hiding place

Ivan Well, I was never much good as a prince. And pedlars go wherever they please.

Vasilisa And they sing.

Firebird (*also putting on a cloak*) And dance.

Ivan (*offering the Tsar a cloak*) And play music.

Tsar Me? But I'm — — (*giving in and taking the cloak*) I'm a pedlar!

They all laugh

Music

Song 10

All (*singing*)   La la la
La la la la la la la
La la la la la la la la
La la la la la la la

Who will buy
A string of shiny buttons
A silver comb a looking glass
A rose of ruby
Who will buy
A roll of silken ribbon
A handkerchief of linen
A golden apple for the one you love

Pedlar girl
Dancing in the moonlight
Dancing in the moonlight
Like a bird of fire
Pedlar girl
Weave your magic story
Weave your magic story
Pedlar girl

Look at me
I'm a wolf with a tooth
And that's no word of a lie
What's the use
Of a wolf with no tooth
A wolf with a tooth am I
Owwwwoooo!
A wolf with a tooth am I

Look at me
I'm a wolf with a tooth
And that's no word of a lie
What's the use
Of a wolf with no tooth
A wolf with a tooth am I
Owwwwoooo
A wolf with a tooth am I

Here comes the Firebird
Blazing Firebird
Blinding Firebird
Here comes the Firebird
Firebird
Setting the heavens aflame
Firebird
Firebird

Here comes the Firebird
Blazing Firebird
Blinding Firebird
Here comes the Firebird

THE END

FURNITURE AND PROPERTY LIST

ACT I

On stage: Forest setting

Off stage: Set elements to make **Tsar**'s palace (**Stage Management**)
Set elements to make garden (**Stage Management**)
Apple tree with gold apples (**Stage Management**)
Rough sign to attach to tree (**Stage Management**)
Set elements to make **Koschei**'s castle interior — including curtained windows, chests of drawers, bottles, potions, books of spells, cushions (**Stage Management**)

Personal: **Pedlar 2**: wolf's tooth on chain
Ivan: coin

ACT II

On stage: INSIDE BABA YAGA'S HUT
Golden cord attaching **Firebird** to **Vanka**
Broom

HIDDEN
Pedlars' cloaks for whole cast

Off stage: Puppets of three galloping horsemen (**Puppeteers**)
Shuttered window unit (**Stage Management**)
Basket of haberdashery (**Vasilisa**)
Gold cloth (**Stage Management**)
Red cloth (**Stage Management**)
Black, star-studded cloth (**Stage Management**)

Personal: **Katya**: tin of polish and cloth

LIGHTING PLOT

Practical fittings required: nil
Various interior and exterior settings

ACT I

To open: Darkness

Cue 1	Music for Song1 begins	(Page 1)
	Bring up general exterior lighting	

Cue 2	**Pedlar 2**: " ... the length and breadth of Russia."	(Page 3)
	*Change to setting for **Tsar**'s garden; daytime*	

Cue 3	**Ivan**: "You can count on us!"	(Page 5)
	Fade lights	

Cue 4	**Katya** and **Ivan** hide near the tree	(Page 6)
	*Bring up lights on **Tsar**'s garden; night-time*	

Cue 5	**Ivan**: "I mustn't let Father down." Music	(Page 6)
	Red glow in the sky	

Cue 6	**Ivan**: "Not yet." Music builds	(Page 6)
	Red glow builds	

Cue 7	**Katya** shrugs off **Ivan**. When ready	(Page 7)
	*Blaze of light on **Firebird***	

Cue 8	The **Firebird** moves away	(Page 9)
	*Fade blaze of light on **Firebird***	

Cue 9	**Katya**: "... my prayers if I were you."	(Page 10)
	Fade lights	

Cue 10	The **Tsar** joins **Katya**	(Page 10)
	*Bring up lights on **Tsar**'s garden; daytime*	

Cue 11	**Ivan** heads out of the palace	(Page 11)
	Lighting change	

Cue 12	The two **Pedlars** exit *Bring lights up on forest*	(Page 12)
Cue 13	**Wolf**: " … and trapped forever." Music *Cross-fade to spot*	(Page 17)
Cue 14	**Ivan** and the **Wolf** exit *Cross-fade to the interior of* **Koschei**'s castle	(Page 17)
Cue 15	**Baba Yaga** enters *Bring up spot on* **Baba Yaga**	(Page 25)
Cue 16	**Baba Yaga** laughs *Black-out*	(Page 25)

ACT II

To open: Darkness

Cue 17	Music Bring up spotlight on **Ivan** and the **Wolf**	(Page 26)
Cue 18	**Ivan**: "Past the golden horseman of day ..." *Bring up lights on puppet horsemen*	(Page 26)
Cue 19	**Wolf**: " … the home of Baba Yaga." *Cut horsemen's light. Bring up general exterior lighting; night-time*	(Page 26)
Cue 20	The exterior of the hut opens up *Bring up lights on hut interior*	(Page 27)
Cue 21	The hut closes up again *Cross-fade to spot on* **Wolf** *and lights on puppet horsemen*	(Page 30)
Cue 22	Third puppet horseman exits *Cut puppet horsemen lights*	(Page 30)
Cue 23	The shutters open *Bring up lights on shuttered window area*	(Page 31)
Cue 24	**Vasilisa**: "Come on. Hurry!"Music *Cross-fade to spot on* **Vasilisa** *and the* **Wolf** *and lights on puppet horsemen*	(Page 31)

Cue 25   Third puppet horseman exits   (Page 31)
            Cut puppet horsemen lights

Cue 26   **Vasilisa** exits   (Page 32)
            Bring up lights on **Baba Yaga***'s hut*

Cue 27   **Baba Yaga** exits   (Page 38)
            Bring up lights on forest

Cue 28   **Ivan**: "What are you doing?"   (Page 40)
            Special lighting effect

Cue 29   **Koschei**:□"— it isn't possible!" Music builds   (Page 40)
            Change lights

Cue 30   **Death** exits; music softens   (Page 40)
            Return lights to forest setting

Cue 31   They all laugh. Music   (Page 42)
            Cross-fade to spot on **Ivan**, **Vasilisa**,
              the **Wolf** *and the* **Firebird**

Cue 32   **Katya** enters the garden wearing gloves   (Page 42)
            Bring up lights on **Tsar***'s garden*

Cue 33   **Firebird**: " — to the fountain of life." Music   (Page 46)
            Change lights for **Firebird***'s flight*

Cue 34   **Firebird** reaches her destination   (Page 46)
            Spectacular fountain of colour and light

Cue 34   **Firebird** returns to the **Tsar**'s garden   (Page 46)
            Return lights to **Tsar***'s garden setting*

EFFECTS PLOT

ACT I

Cue 1   Music fades   (Page 6)
               Owl hoots

Cue 2   **The Firebird** circles the apple tree   (Page 7)
               Recorded **Chorus** *sings Song 2*

Cue 3   **Ivan** watches the **Firebird** go   (Page 9)
               Recorded **Chorus** *sings Song 2 reprise*

Cue 4   **Vasilisa**: " … that's made of wood?"   (Page 20)
               Koschei*'s voice-over; dialogue as p. 20*
               OR ensure offstage microphone is live
               Echo effect on closing words and laughter

ACT II

Cue 5   **Ivan** pushes the door open   (Page 27)
               Squeak